THE TALE OF THE LUCKY CAT

まねき猫の話

Retold and illustrated by

SUNNY SEKI

文と絵　サニー関

East West Discovery Press

Manhattan Beach, California

This book is dedicated to my parents, brother, wife, nine children, and our cat.
- S.S

Text and illustrations copyright © 2007 by East West Discovery Press
Japanese translation copyright © 2007 by East West Discovery Press

Published by:
East West Discovery Press
P.O. Box 3585, Manhattan Beach, CA 90266
Phone: 310-545-3730, Fax: 310-545-3731
Website: www.eastwestdiscovery.com

Written and illustrated by Sunny Seki
Edited by Marcie Rouman
Book production by Luzelena Rodriguez
Production management by Icy Smith

ISBN-13: 978-0-9669437-5-7 Hardcover
Library of Congress Control Number: 2007938121
First Bilingual English and Japanese Edition 2007
Printed in China
Published in the United States of America

The Tale of the Lucky Cat is also available in English only and eight bilingual editions including English with Arabic, Chinese, Hmong, Japanese, Korean, Spanish, Tagalog and Vietnamese.

Japanese Glossary:
Tama: A round object
Sensei: A respectful word for teacher
Osho: Leader of a Buddhist temple
Osho-san: The respectful and friendly way to address the *osho*
Kokoro: The mind or spirit of a living thing
Maneki: Inviting or beckoning
Neko: Cat

A long time ago in Japan, there lived a toymaker named Tokuzo. He was a kind
young man who traveled from village to village to sell his toys at festivals.

むかし　日本に　おもちゃ屋さんの　とくぞうという人がいました。村のお祭りで
おもちゃを　売り歩く　きだてのやさしい若者でした。

Children liked his toys. Still, Tokuzo was making barely enough money to survive. "Someday," he thought, "I'll create something so unique that everyone will want to have it."

おもちゃは　ときどき売れますが、とくぞうには　やっと生活できる　お金しか入ってきません。
「いつか‥‥　皆が喜こぶおもちゃを作りたいなあ」というのが　彼の夢でした。

The next festival was big, and Tokuzo knew that he would be able to sell a lot of toys there. So he was in a hurry to get the best place. He started on his journey, but had no idea that soon his life was about to change.

次の　お祭りは大きいので　早く着き、良い場所を取ろうと　急いで　いたときの
ことです。人生は何が待っているか、誰にもわかりません。

He had just entered a small village, when suddenly a frightened cat darted past him. It was being chased by a growling dog.

"Oh, no! Stop!" Tokuzo screamed because he saw an express-delivery horse speeding in their direction. He stood helplessly as the horse hit the cat.

町中へきたとき、おびえた猫が　彼のわきを　かけ抜けてゆきました。うなり声を
あげた犬に　追いかけられていたのです。

「あっ、あぶない。止まれ！」とくぞうは、早馬が　かけてくるのを見て
さけびました。しかし、馬が猫を　はねてしまうのを　どうすることも
できませんでした。

The accident happened so quickly that the townspeople did not notice the cat at all. But Tokuzo saw that it had been badly hurt.

"Maybe I can save it. It's still breathing," he said. He quickly found an inn, and carried the cat inside.

あっという間(ま)のことで、
町(まち)の人は猫(ねこ)に気(き)がつきません。
でも, とくぞうは　けがを
した猫(ねこ)が　心配(しんぱい)です。
　「まだ息(いき)があるから、助(たす)け
られるかもしれない」と
近(ちか)くの宿屋(やどや)に　猫(ねこ)をつれて
ゆきました。

That night, Tokuzo stayed up late. He wrapped the cat's broken leg and made sure that the bed was warm and clean. "I'll name you 'Tama' – just like the round bell you are wearing," said Tokuzo.

その夜、とくぞうは おそくまで 猫の手あてをしました。折れた足に ささえをつけ、寝どこは気持ちよく ととのえます。

「首に鈴をつけているので おまえを『タマ』と呼ぶことにしよう」と 声をかけました。

The next morning, Tama opened its eyes and seemed to smile.

"Good, Tama. I am so relieved. Today is the big festival, but I'm going to stay behind in this small town with you instead. I want to be sure that you get well."

朝になって タマは目を開け、にっこりしたようでした。

「よしよし タマ ひと安心だ。きょうは お祭りにゆくかわり、この町にいて おまえが良くなったら 出かけよう」と とくぞうははげましたのです。

The following day, Tokuzo was able to sell a few toys to the village children. With the little money he earned, he bought two fish: one for himself, and one for Tama. "Tonight we'll celebrate!" he thought.

He returned to the inn and opened the door. "Tama..." he called. However, when he lit the candle, he discovered that Tama had died.

その日、町で少しかせいだお金で　二ひきの魚（自分とタマに一匹ずつ）を買いました。「今夜は　タマが良くなったお祝いだ」と　いうつもりです。
宿屋にかえり　戸を開けて「タマ・・・」と呼びかけ　ろうそくに火をつけたとき、
タマは　すでに　死んで　つめたくなっていました。

The next morning, Tokuzo buried Tama in a grave overlooking the broad countryside.
His heart was heavy with grief as he said goodbye.

つぎの日の朝、とくぞうは　町はずれの丘に　お墓をつくり　タマを　うめました。
「さようなら」彼は　かなしさで　いっぱいです。

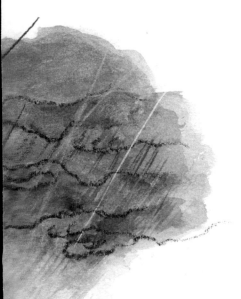

The big festival was almost over, but Tokuzo still had time. So he continued on his journey. Suddenly the sky grew dark. Rumbling thunder warned that a rainstorm was coming fast.

お祭りに間にあいそうなので　急いで歩いていると、
暗くなって　雷 が鳴り　嵐 がきそうです。

He quickly ran to the closest tree for cover. The rain started to pour harder and harder.

とくぞうが　近くの木の下にかけこむと同時に、雨は　どんどん
はげしく降ってきました。

As Tokuzo wiped his face, he noticed a cat meowing by the temple gate. It seemed to be inviting him to come inside! Surprisingly, this cat looked like Tama, who had died just the day before.

木の下で 体をふいていると、道のむこうで 猫の鳴き声がします。見ると お寺のほうへ 来るように 手まねきしているではありませんか！

驚いたことに、その猫は きのう死んだタマに そっくりです。

Tokuzo forgot about the rain. He ran toward the cat. "Tama, Tama… is that you? What are you doing here? I thought you died!" He had almost touched the cat, when suddenly…

とくぞうは　雨も わすれて　猫へ　かけよりました。「タマ、タマ、おまえさん、死んだはずなのに　そこで　何をしているの？」もう少しで　手が 届くとき・・・

BAM! There was a huge explosion of light and sound. He turned around and gasped. The pine tree that had protected him from the rain had been split in half by a powerful bolt of lightning!

「ピカッ、ドカーン！」　稲光と大音響に　ふり返ったとくぞうは　声も出ません。雨やどりしていた松は　雷が落ちて　まっ二つです。

Tokuzo told everyone how a mysterious cat had saved him. The people were amazed at this story. They could not believe it. "How can cats know that lightning is going to strike? And if cats are dead, how can they call you?"

Tokuzo did not know how to answer. "I am sure that cat saved my life, but I have no way to prove it to you."

The *Osho-San* was listening carefully at the temple. "Maybe there is some truth here that we cannot explain. Tokuzo, please spend the night with us at the temple so that we can talk about it."

とくぞうは　皆に　ふしぎな猫に　すくわれた　話をしました。しかし　誰も
信じません。「雷がおちると　猫にわかるかね？それに　死んだ猫が　手まねき
できるはずがない」

とくぞうは　困りました。「残念ながら　私は　あの猫に　すくわれたと
証明までは　できません」

和尚さんは　まじめに聞き「世の中には　説明できないこともある。とくぞうさん
お寺にとまって、もう少し　話をしてゆきなさい」と　すすめました。

18

He went to the meditation garden to think. "I was saved by Tama, and the people didn't believe it. What am I supposed to do next? I should create a statue of this cat," he thought, "so everybody can share my good luck."

He asked the *osho-san* for advice. "Let me introduce you to Old Master Craftsman. His daughter takes care of him because he is not well. But he is wise, and will tell you what you should do."

お寺の庭で座禅をしつつ、とくぞうは これからについて 考えました。タマの話は 忘れられない強烈 なものです。「そうだ！ あの猫の像を作ろう。タマの記念にもなり、みんなに幸運を与えられる」と 考えつきました。

和尚さんに 意見を求めると「それならば 陶芸の名人に 紹介してあげよう。いま 彼は病気で 娘さんが面倒をみているが、りっぱな人だから 助けてくれるだろう」という返事です。

Old Master Craftsman was not feeling well, but he was happy to give Tokuzo some advice. "Clay is the best material for your statues, and my workshop has everything you will need. You are welcome to stay there. Unfortunately, you'll have to work by yourself, because I am too sick to help you."

名人は寝たままで「ねん土を使いなさい。私の仕事小屋に　必要なものはそろっている。悪いが　私は病気なので　自分でやりなさい」と言いました。

Tokuzo opened the workshop door. Where could he begin? Tools and supplies were everywhere! He felt lost, but at the same time very excited.

仕事小屋の　戸から　のぞくと，道具や材料が　いっぱいで　こんがらがりそう。心ぼそいけれど、やりがいも　ありそうです。

He started to follow Old
Master's directions. First, he had
to mix the clay.

名人の言ったとうり、
まず　ねん土を　こねます。

Then, he had to form it into the shape of
a cat. "These don't look like cats at all!" he
told himself.

それを　猫の　形　にするのが　むずかしい。
「どうも猫らしくならないなあ」と
つい　ひとりごとが　出てしまいます。

Next, the clay had to be baked so that it
could harden. But to start a fire, first wood
had to be cut. This was much more work
than he had expected.

つぎは　焼きがまに入れ　固くします。
それには　木を切って、火を　おこさねば
なりません。まきわりは　思ったより
大変な仕事でした。

23

Finally, the clay was baked! Tokuzo reached for the oven door, and peered down at his work. He couldn't believe his eyes. "Look at my cats! What did I do wrong?" His carefully formed statues had cracked and shattered into pieces.

ついに　でき上（あが）り！　ところが　焼（や）きがまの戸（と）をあけて　びっくり。
「どこで　　まちがったんだろう。大失敗（だいしっぱい）だ！」　猫（ねこ）の像（ぞう）は　ヒビがはいり　割（わ）れていたのです。

He brought his work to Old Master Craftsman. "This can be a nice-looking cat, young man. But you did not mix the clay well, and the fire was too hot," he said.

Tokuzo would not give up. He needed more firewood, so he went back to the tree that had been struck by lightning. He started over again, and worked day and night.

名人に見せにゆくと「もうちょっとで 良くなるぞ。ただ もっと ねん土を こねるように、火が熱すぎないように 気をつけなさい」と注意をされました。

とくぞうは あきらめません。もっと まきがいるので 雷 が おちた木を もらいにゆきました。すべてやりなおし、昼も夜も はたらきます。

25

One fine morning, Old Master was feeling a little better. and he came out to watch. He was impressed by Tokuzo's determination. "Your cats are looking much better. Now, why don't you make the arm swing by hiding a weight inside the body?" he asked. "The cleverest ideas are often hidden behind what the eye can see."

Tokuzo jumped up, amazed. "Yes! That will make the cat seem more alive. Thank you so much, *Sensei*!" Now Old Master started to get excited, too.

ある晴れた日、名人は　気分が少しよくなり　仕事を見にきました。
とくぞうの　熱意に　感心してのことです。「ずいぶんと　良くなったな。
ところで　おもりを　猫の中にいれて、手をふれるようにしたら　どうだろう。
すぐれた仕かけは　見えない所　にするものだ」と教えました。
　とくぞうは大喜び。「それは良い。猫が生きているようでしょうね。
先生　ありがとう！」こうして　名人も　完成を楽しみにしだしたのです。

A few weeks later, Tokuzo perfected
his cat. "Look, everyone! I did it! My
dream has finally come true!"

Old Master Craftsman came running from
his bed. "Good job! You did it!" he exclaimed.

His daughter was cheering, too. "How wonderful! My
father is running without his cane! Tokuzo, your cat has
chased his pain away!"

何週間かたって、とくぞうは 猫を仕上げました。「皆さん どうぞ 見て
ください。ついに夢が かないました」

名人は ふとんから 飛び出してきました。「よくやった！とくぞう」

娘 さんも 歓声をあげています。「まあ 何とすばらしいんでしょう。
おとうさんが 杖もいらずに 走っているなんて。とくぞうさんの猫が 病気を
追い出してしまった！」

It happened that Old Master's daughter was a talented painter. So she helped decorate the statues. "This cat has a whole new life of its own!" Tokuzo was thrilled. They named the cat *Maneki Neko,* which means "The Cat That Invites Good Luck."

娘 さんは絵がうまく、色をつける手伝いをしてくれます。とくぞうは
「それぞれが　生きているみたいだ」と目をみはりました。
彼らは　この猫を『まねき猫』（幸 せをまねく猫）と名ずけました。

Soon, *Maneki Neko* statues spread all over Japan, and everybody wanted to have one. As time passed, people started to say that a raised right paw brings fortune, and a raised left paw brings happiness and good luck.

「まねき猫」は　日本中にひろまり、皆が欲しがりました。やがて

猫の右手はお金をまねく、左手は幸せを呼ぶ　と言われるようになったのです。

"*Osho-san*, did Tama really die?" Old Master asked.

"Well, the body can die, but the *kokoro* lives forever. Therefore, Tama can always remain in our hearts."

This story of the *Maneki Neko* reminds us that what we do is the cause of tomorrow. Even a tiny kitten might remember what we do. And it might even save our life. Or it might just be a friend forever and ever.

「和尚さん、タマは死んだのでしょうかね？」と名人がたずねました。

「さあて、体は死んでも　心は永遠じゃ。タマは皆の気持ちの中に生き続けるであろうなあ」と和尚さんは答えたそうです。

この話は　今日したことが　明日を作る、と教えてくれます。仔猫でも私たちが　したことを覚えていて　命を救ってくれるかも知れません。

あるいは　いつまでも　友だちでいてくれることでしょう。